Willow

Illustrator/Artist: Pettina Velez
Author: John Velez

AuthorHouse™
1663 Liberty Drive
Bloomington, IN 47403
www.authorhouse.com
Phone: 833-262-8899

Interior Image Credit: Pettina Velez

This book is printed on acid-free paper.

ISBN: 979-8-8230-1384-0 (sc)
ISBN: 979-8-8230-1386-4 (hc)
ISBN: 979-8-8230-1385-7 (e)

Print information available on the last page.

Published by AuthorHouse 08/29/2023

authorHOUSE®

Dedication

This book is dedicated to our Grandchildren and all the kids that Pettina has cared for over the years. Special thanks goes to Pettina's sweet sister and Constant critic.

2

Good Morning Kitty!
It's such a beautiful day!
Guess what?
Today is our Halloween party!!

"I love this pumpkin dress!" Says Willow.

"Willow, its time for breakfast!"

"Ok Mom, I'll be right there!"

Good morning!
Thanks Mom, I love French toast!
Do you like French toast, Ben?

"It's time to put up the Halloween decorations for our party!" Says Willow.

"Mom, Ben wants to help too!"
(Knock, knock)
"Oh! Someone is at the door! , I'll get it!"

"Hi Annie!"
"Hi Willow, do you want to come out and play?"
"Ok, let me clean up my mess first."

"Hey Annie, what are you going to dress up as for Halloween?"

"(Hee, Hee, Hee) It's a surprise!"

"What about you Willow?"

"Mine's a surprise too!"

"I love Fall and all the beautiful Colors, I think that it's my favorite time of year!"
"Me too! I love to play in the leaves!" Says Annie.

"I'm so excited for your Halloween
party tonight!" Says Annie.
"Me too!" Says Willow.
"It's going to be so much fun to go
Trick or Treating afterwards!"
"Thanks for coming over, see you later tonight!"

TRICK OR TREAT Bags

APPLE Bobbing

20

"Mom? Is it almost time for my friends to arrive?"

"Soon, very soon". Says Mom.

"These apples and all these treats look so yummy!"

"Can we turn on some spooky music now?"

(Ding, Dong)

"Hi guys, Come on in!"

"You all look so great!"

"Welcome to our Halloween party!"

"Decorating our Halloween bags was such a good idea and so much fun!" Says Annie.

"Gus, your bag looks so scary!" Says Willow.

"Great! Thanks! It's supposed to be!" Says Gus.

"Mary, yours looks so cool!" Says Willow.

"Thanks!" Says Mary.

"Jose, yours looks so funny, I love it!" Says Annie,

(Music playing)

"I love the Monster Mash!" Says Mary.

"My favorite is the theme to the Addams Family!" Says Willow.

"Ok kids, it's time to go Trick or Treating." Says Mom.

"YEAH!!" says the kids.

"Don't forget your Halloween bags and remember, we don't eat any treats until we get back home." Says Willow.

"The Jack O Lanterns look so cool and all the Halloween decorations look so spooky!"

"I love the house with the giant pumpkin!" Says Jose.

"My favorite is the house with all the scary bats!" Says Gus.

"The one with the skeleton in the tree was my favorite!" Says Annie.

"TRICK OR TREAT!"

"Oh my!! You all look so great!!"

"Thank you Mrs. Brewster!" The kids all say.

"My Trick or Treat bag is getting
really heavy!" Says Mary.

"Yeah! I guess it's time to go home." Says Jose.

"Thanks Willow, this night was
the best!" Says Gus.

"Thanks Mom for letting me and my friends have the Halloween party and go out Trick or Treating! This was the best Halloween ever!!" Says Willow. HAPPY HALLOWEEN EVERYONE!!

We have both collaborated and ventured into the world of children's books. This book is a second collection of Pettina's hand paintings.

Pettina has been a full time professional nanny for over 20 years. She loves reading and teaching art to children.

John, Pettina's husband, is a full time Landscape Designer and Pettina's biggest fan.

We live in San Carlos, CA with our two Chihuahuas, Emma and kitty and our faithful Parrot, Watson.

Printed in the United States
by Baker & Taylor Publisher Services